W9-BZU-080

5-Minute Under the Sea Stories

DISNEY PRESS
Los Angeles • New York

Collection copyright © 2020 Disney Enterprises, Inc. All rights reserved. Pixar properties © Disney/Pixar.

"Who Needs a Hug?" written by Beth Sycamore. Copyright © 2017 Disney Enterprises, Inc., and Pixar.

"Ariel and the Pearl of Wisdom" written by Thea Feldman. Copyright © 2019 Disney Enterprises, Inc.

"A Path to the Sea" written by Osnat Shurer. Copyright © 2018 Disney Enterprises, Inc.

"You're It, Dory!" adapted by Lauren Clauss from the original story written by Bonita Garr. Copyright © 2016 Disney Enterprises, Inc., and Pixar.

"Becoming Shiny" written by Brittany Rubiano. Copyright © 2017 Disney Enterprises, Inc.

"Ariel Makes Waves" written by Liz Marsham. Copyright © 2017 Disney Enterprises, Inc.

"Lilo and Stitch" adapted by Catherine Hapka. Copyright © 2002 Disney Enterprises, Inc.

"Pua and Heihei" written by Suzanne Francis. Copyright © 2016 Disney Enterprises, Inc.

"Night Games" written by Elizabeth Rudnick. Copyright © 2016 Disney Enterprises, Inc., and Pixar.

"Ariel and the Whale Song" adapted by Hannah Eliot from the original story "Ariel and the Big Baby" written by Amy Sky Koster. Copyright © 2015 Disney Enterprises, Inc.

"The Ghost-Light Fish" written by Laura Driscoll. Copyright © 2006 Disney Enterprises, Inc., and Pixar.

"Wave Rider" written by Osnat Shurer. Copyright © 2018 Disney Enterprises, Inc.

All illustrations by the Disney Storybook Art Team

Published by Disney Press, an imprint of Disney Book Group. No part of this book may be reproduced or transmitted in any form or by any means, electronic or mechanical, including photocopying, recording, or by any information storage and retrieval system, without written permission from the publisher.

For information address Disney Press, 1200 Grand Central Avenue, Glendale, California 91201.

Printed in the United States of America

First Hardcover Edition, May 2020

Library of Congress Control Number: 2019908376

1 3 5 7 9 10 8 6 4 2

ISBN 978-1-368-05552-9

FAC-038091-20094

For more Disney Press fun, visit www.disneybooks.com

SUSTAINABLE FORESTRY INITIATIVE
Certified Sourcing
www.sfiprogram.org
SFI-00993
Logo Applies to Text Stock Only

Contents

Who Needs a Hug?

Dory darted across the sandy floor in front of her parents' home in Morro Bay. She noticed a purple shell and gently tossed it high over her head.

Dory smiled.

"I like shells. And Mom loves purple ones," she said.

Jenny and Charlie swam out of their home to meet Dory. Dory couldn't wait to show off the reef and her coral cave to her mom and dad. And they couldn't wait to move in.

"I'm so happy we're together," said Jenny. "I think I need a hug. A great big, oh-so-tight family hug." Dory, Charlie, and Jenny snuggled up to each other.

"You know who gives great hugs?" Dory asked. "Nemo! I wonder what he's up to. I'd better go find him." Dory turned and swam off into the bay to find Nemo.

Dory swam through the dark green kelp. She spied Nemo playing hide-and-seek with some new friends.

"Hey, what's wrong with your fin?" the angelfish asked Nemo. "It's so tiny."

Nemo looked down at his fin. He didn't think it looked wrong.

Dory swam over. "That tiny fin took Nemo across the entire Pacific Ocean," she said. "He's one of the best swimmers I know."

"I think you need a
hug, you super-duper
swimmer," Dory
said. She gave
Nemo a heartfelt
squeeze.

"Come play
with us, Dory!"
Nemo said. "You're
it, so start counting!"
Dory started to count.

But soon she noticed
some shells and started
counting them instead.
She bumped into a
giant stalk of kelp
and saw something
wriggling near the
surface. A small
ball of fur was
looking down at her.
"Well, hello
there!" Dory said.

Meanwhile, Nemo and his friends waited for Dory to find them. They waited and waited and waited.

"I think Dory forgot about us," Nemo said. "We should go find her."

The three fish swam out from their hiding spots and found Dory. She was staring at something up in the kelp.

"Look! It's a baby otter," said the angelfish.

"Yay! One more player!" shouted Nemo. "Let's hide! Don't forget, Dory. You need to look for us."

Nemo and his friends swam off again. The baby otter wriggled out of the seaweed. He dove and splashed in the water. He couldn't wait to hide.

Dory began to count. "Ten, nine, eight . . . twelve, eleven, ten . . . three, two, one . . . Ready or not, here I come!"

Dory darted this way and that way. She found Nemo in a group
of sea urchins. She found the angelfish and the parrot
fish hiding behind some rocks.

"My turn! It's my turn to hide!" Dory shouted.

Nemo looked around. "But where's the otter?
Did you find him?"

"Oh, that cute little brown ball of fur . . .
Well . . . um . . . no," Dory admitted.

"If he's lost, you can find him, Dory!" Nemo said. "When I was lost, you helped my dad find me. You never gave up."

"You can count on me," said Dory as she darted off to find the otter. Nemo and his friends raced after her. The otter wasn't under the tall red buoy or the large gray rock. Then Dory spotted something up ahead.

"Look! Over there—that looks like an otter!" she shouted.

But it wasn't the little otter. It was Destiny and Bailey. Destiny suddenly bumped into something soft and squishy. A cloud of black ink spread through the water. It was Hank! Hank blushed and sank down to hide.

"I'm sorry, Hank," whispered Destiny. "I didn't mean to scare you. Do you need a hug?"

"Me? Hug? Nah," grumbled Hank as he pushed Destiny away. Hank noticed everyone staring at him.

"Hank's worried about looking silly," explained Nemo. "But accidents happen to all of us."

"I get a little embarrassed when I bump into things," admitted Destiny. "I'm not a great swimmer."

"Yes, you are!" Dory assured her friend. "You swim beautifully."

"Let's go," said Nemo. "We need to find the otter and get him back home before his parents worry."

"Can I help?" asked Destiny.

"Ooh-ooh! Me too!" shouted Bailey.

Dory asked Bailey to use his echolocation to help find the otter. Bailey put his flippers to his head.

"OOOOOOOOOOO. I think it's working," he said. "He's in the kelp forest. Go straight and then left."

"Excellent work, Bailey!" said Dory as she gave his flipper a quick squeeze.

Thanks to Bailey, they soon found the otter pup sound asleep on a kelp bed.

"Awww," sighed Nemo. "Poor little guy probably got tired of waiting to be found and fell asleep."

"Let's get you back home," Dory whispered to the otter pup. Destiny slowly glided upward and gently lifted the sleeping otter out of the water.

Bailey swam ahead to guide Destiny as she carried the otter pup closer to shore.

"Go right, then left, Destiny," Bailey called out as he navigated.

When they swam around the last rock, otters were everywhere! Some were chasing each other in the water. Some were diving for food. And a few were dozing on their backs.

The familiar sounds woke up the otter pup. He squealed and jumped into the water. Dory saw him swim to two other otters on the rocks.

"Those must be his parents!" she said.

The little otter and his parents embraced in a huge otter family hug. They had missed their otter pup! They couldn't hug him enough.

Moments later, the sun began to set over the bay. All the otters moved in closer. One by one, they placed their arms around each other and began to hug. It was a giant cuddle party.

Dory and her friends gathered together. Charlie, Jenny, and Marlin surfaced beside them.

"That's one big happy family," said Hank.

Dory sighed. She remembered how much she loved her friends
and family.

"I think I need a hug," she said.

Everyone—even Hank—gathered around Dory. They placed
their fins, flippers, and arms around her and hugged.

Ariel and the Pearl of Wisdom

It was the night before the Pearl of Wisdom ceremony. Ariel was excited! On that special day King Triton's daughters would each take on an official royal responsibility.

The day would begin in the morning when each princess selected a pearl from the palace's pearl room to mark the occasion. In the afternoon, there would be a ceremony to announce how each of them planned to help Atlantica.

"What are you going to do?" Andrina asked Ariel.

"I don't know yet," Ariel said. "I need to figure that out before the ceremony tomorrow."

In the pearl room the next morning, each princess chose her favorite pearl.

"I look forward to hearing what you've chosen as your gifts to the kingdom!" King Triton said, hugging each daughter. "May these pearls be a reminder of your royal responsibility."

After everyone had left, Ariel swam to her grotto to think about how she could help the kingdom. Her collection always made her happy. She loved her objects from the human world, and thanks to Scuttle, she knew that each one had a purpose—and a story.

Flounder appeared. "I'm so excited about your special day!" he said.

But Ariel wasn't listening. She had spotted something partially hidden in the sand and hurried to uncover it. "We have to show it to Scuttle!" she said.

"Ariel!" cried Flounder. "Maybe today is not the day to go to the surface!"

"Don't be such a guppy!" Ariel responded. "What could go wrong?"

When Ariel found Scuttle, she showed him her new treasure. Scuttle examined the object closely.

"I know!" he declared. "This here is a thingamajiggy! And you wear it . . . *here*!" Scuttle reached for Ariel's seaweed necklace and hung the object on it.

But the object was so heavy it ripped the necklace right off Ariel's neck. The pearl, the seaweed chain, and the thingamajiggy all sank.

"Oh, no!" Ariel shouted. She waved a quick good-bye to Scuttle as she and Flounder dove beneath the surface.

Ariel looked around frantically. She had to find
that pearl.

"Look, Flounder! There it is!" Ariel shouted.
They watched the pearl as it hit a starfish
napping on a rock.

The starfish swatted it away without even waking up, and the pearl flew through the water.

Now it was headed toward an octopus. As Ariel and Flounder chased after it, the pearl landed on one of the octopus's arms.

"Wait! Stop!" Ariel shouted.

When the octopus saw Ariel waving to him, he was so delighted he waved back—with all eight of his arms!

The pearl flew loose and sank out of sight as the octopus continued on his way.

"Oh, Flounder," Ariel sighed. "I've lost the pearl! What am I going to do? How will I ever explain this?"

Suddenly, Sebastian appeared. "I've been looking for you everywhere!" he cried.

Ariel could not believe her eyes. There, behind his head, was the pearl!

"Young lady," Sebastian scolded, "you need to get back to the palace right now!"

"Whatever you say, Sebastian," said Ariel, smiling. She leaned toward him—and kissed him! As the crab blushed, Ariel quickly plucked up the pearl without him noticing.

The three swam back to the palace. Ariel clutched
the pearl tightly in her hand, vowing to take
better care of it.

At the palace, Ariel made a visit to the royal jeweler
for a new chain. It was time for the ceremony.

After her sisters made their announcements, it was Ariel's turn. Ariel knew exactly what to say.

"I am going to start a new museum dedicated to collecting and displaying beautiful sea art in all its forms," Ariel announced. The entire kingdom cheered and applauded.

"You have made a wise choice, Ariel," King Triton said,
"one in keeping with your generous nature. Today you and your
sisters have shone brighter than any pearl ever could."

On opening day of the museum, Ariel couldn't have been prouder
to showcase some of the beauty found under the sea.

A Path to the Sea

Moana loved the ocean. When she was old enough, Gramma Tala taught her how to surf, and she spent a lot of time trying to ride the waves.

After paddling into the ocean, Moana would float on her board and wait. Then, when the right wave came along, she would pop up and stand on her surfboard. It was challenging for Moana to keep her balance as a little wave carried her to shore, but when she could, riding waves was so much fun!

One day, as Moana and Pua waited for a wave, a sea turtle paddled toward Moana and looked right at her. "Hello," she said.

There was something familiar about the sea turtle, but Moana couldn't figure out where or when she had met him before. It was almost as if she'd known him when she was a little girl.

The sea turtle stayed with Moana and Pua, playing with them in the water all day long. Moana named the turtle Lolo. When the sun started to set, Moana lifted her surfboard out of the water. "Bye, Lolo," she said, feeling only a little sad. Somehow, she knew she would see her friend again.

For many days, whenever Moana and Pua went to the ocean, Lolo found them. They had fun swimming, surfing, and playing in the waves.

Moana stayed on the shore until dark to watch the ocean sparkle in the moonlight.

"I knew I would find you here," said Gramma Tala, joining Moana on the beach. Moana noticed Lolo swimming toward the shore.

They watched as the sea turtle crawled up on the sand and over toward the coconut trees. There, Lolo started digging a hole.

"What is he doing, Gramma?" asked Moana.

"*She*, you mean," Gramma Tala said with a laugh.

"Your turtle friend just laid her eggs in the hole she dug," Gramma Tala said. "Those are nesting grounds. Generations of sea turtles lay their eggs right there." She told Moana how the baby turtles made their way to the ocean after hatching. "And when the females grow up, they come back here to lay their eggs."

"How do they remember that spot?" Moana asked. "And how do the babies even know to go into the ocean?"

"They just know," said Gramma Tala.

After that night, Moana checked the nesting grounds every day. She wondered when the baby turtles would hatch and hoped she would get to see them.

One day, Moana and Pua were surfing when the sky turned gray. As the rain poured down, they raced back to the village.

When they got home, they watched the trees bend and sway as they listened to the music of the raindrops.

Soon after the storm was over, Moana grabbed her surfboard and hurried back to the ocean. When she got there, she couldn't believe her eyes: the storm had knocked a coconut tree right on top of the nesting grounds! Fortunately, the eggs were safely buried deep underground. *But what if the baby sea turtles hatch?* she wondered. *They could be trapped!* Moana had to do something fast.

She ran back to the village and told her friends what had happened. "The eggs will hatch any day," she explained.

Her friends agreed to help, and Moana led them to the site.

They all worked together to carefully move the fallen tree.
But then they heard a loud crack! Another palm tree had been
damaged in the storm, and it was about to fall onto the nesting grounds!

"Hurry!" urged Moana. "Let's push it away from the nest."
Everyone gathered around the broken tree. They used all their
strength to push until it finally snapped and fell—far away from the nest.
"We did it!" cheered Moana, breathing a big sigh of relief.

The next day, Moana and Gramma Tala were dancing with the ocean waves when Moana saw something move in the nesting grounds. "Gramma, look!" she shouted.

Lolo's eggs were hatching! Moana watched as the baby sea turtles started to wiggle and move, and soon they began to make their way to the ocean.

When a seabird swooped in and tried to capture one of the baby turtles, Moana waved a palm leaf and Pua chased the bird away. Moana and her friends protected the newborns, determined to see that each and every one made it safely to the water.

Once the turtle babies were all safely swimming, Moana grabbed her surfboard. As she and Pua glided out, Lolo and her babies swam around them, paddling and playing together.

Moana smiled. She felt great knowing that she had helped them. And there was no better way to celebrate than by enjoying the ocean together.

You're It, Dory!

After school, Nemo, Marlin, Dory, and all their friends decided to play a game of hide-and-seek. Dory was it first! Everyone swam to find a hiding place as she began to count.

"One . . . two . . . three . . . um . . . four . . . um . . . um . . ." Dory counted.

When Dory opened her eyes, she forgot why she was counting!

"Hmmm, what was I about to do? Lie and sneak? No. Why would I do that? Spy and peek? No . . . that can't be right. Oh! Hide and seek!" she said, swimming toward Nemo and Marlin's anemone, hoping to find them there.

But by the time Dory got to their anemone, she'd forgotten why she went. She had a nagging feeling she shouldn't get *too* close, but she couldn't remember why. . . .

"YEEOWCH!" she exclaimed. "Now I remember. I'm not supposed to touch anemones because they sting!"

As she swam away, Marlin and Nemo peeked out from their anemone.

"Where's she going, Dad?" Nemo asked. "She was so close to finding us!"

"I'm not sure . . ." Marlin responded.

"Hmmm, what was I doing again?" Dory asked herself. She tried her best to remember, but she kept getting distracted and swimming past all her friends.

"My spot is so good!" Pearl whispered to Sheldon after Dory swam by.

"Mine too! I love hide-and-seek!" Sheldon whispered back.

Dory even swam past Mr. Ray! She was so excited to see a large patch of pristine sand to squish and play with that she completely missed him hiding beneath it! Mr. Ray smiled, proud of his clever hiding place.

"Wait! Wasn't I playing hide-and-seek?" Dory said, finally remembering.

"Wow, that guy looks a lot like Hank," Dory said. "What color is he again? Yellow? No. Pink? Nope, I don't think so. Blue?"

Dory continued to swim through the coral field, and Hank tried his best to blend in with his surroundings as she got closer to him.

"That was a close call," Hank said to himself when Dory eventually swam away, still on the hunt for friends.

But as Dory swam through the Great Barrier Reef, she again forgot she was playing hide-and-seek.

She swam past Bailey, who was hiding behind some seaweed, and she swam right *over* Destiny, who was hiding on the ocean floor!

As Dory kept swimming, she spotted a beautiful purple shell. "My mom loves shells!" she said. "I should give this one to her. But I haven't seen my mom or dad in a while. Actually, I haven't seen any of my friends. Where are they?"

That's when Dory remembered they were playing hide-and-seek . . .
but not that she was it!

"Uh-oh, I'd better hide quick!" she said.

Dory's parents, Charlie and Jenny, watched from
their hiding place as Dory swam into a nearby
cave. They expected her to come out once
she realized no one was there, but
after a couple of minutes, they
started to worry.

They decided to abandon the game and go check on their daughter. Luckily, they found her right away.

"Kelpcake, what are you up to?" Charlie said.

"Mom! Dad! We're playing hide-and-seek, and I found this *great* hiding spot! Come in, I'll make room," Dory told them.

"But, sweetie—" Jenny tried to explain that everyone was hiding from Dory, but before she could, Dory dashed to the opening of the cave.

Hank and Mr. Ray were swimming past the cave and wanted to help them hide, too. "Okay, okay, everybody in. We can squeeze," she said.

"But, Dory—" Mr. Ray began, but before he could get another word out, Dory saw even more of her friends in need of a hiding spot.

It wasn't long before the cave was packed. Nearly everyone who was supposed to be hiding from Dory was in the cave with her!

"It's gonna be tight," she said. "Destiny, suck it in a bit. Watch your head, Bailey!"

Finally, Nemo and Marlin wandered into the cave. They were shocked to find all their friends crowded in with Dory!

"Dory," Nemo said, "what are you doing?"

"Nemo! We are . . . hmmm . . . What *are* we doing?"

"Playing hide-and-seek!" everyone shouted.

The group swam out of the cave as Nemo explained what had happened.

"But you're it, Dory. You're supposed to be looking for *us*."

"Oh, I see. . . . Found you!" Dory exclaimed.

Marlin had a solution. "Let's just play tag."

Becoming Shiny

Moana loved gathering the village children and telling them a story, just like her Gramma Tala used to do.

"Tell us another!" a little boy said.

"A scary one from your adventures," a girl chimed in. "One about . . . Lalotai!"

Moana smiled. "Oh, you want to hear about the realm of the monsters, huh?" she said, then started the story.

"When Maui and I were on our adventure to return the heart of Te Fiti, we visited Lalotai. There we met a giant crab monster named Tamatoa. You see, Tamatoa is a collector of all types of treasures—especially shiny ones. He had Maui's fishhook! We had to get it back.

"Wait!" a little boy cried out. "Why does Tamatoa like shiny things?"

Moana considered this. She thought about what the crab monster had told her and the legends she'd learned about him since. "Well, Tamatoa thought he could make himself beautiful by putting shiny things on his shell. He believed that outer beauty was more important than inner beauty."

"He believed this even when he was growing up. Monsters, like Tamatoa, liked to hear scary stories, too. But their stories were always about Maui! He'd defeated so many monsters that a lot of them were afraid of him. And everyone knew two things about the demigod: that he had a powerful fishhook and that he was covered in magical tattoos.

"Maui inspired little Tamatoa. He wanted to be feared by everyone, too, including the demigod. But to be the most amazing monster in all of Lalotai, he needed something to set him apart.

"'What I need,' Tamatoa told himself, 'is a *look*.'

"So Tamatoa went about finding one. He tried covering himself with rocks, kelp, and even prickly urchins. But nothing worked.

"Until," Moana continued, "one fateful day, something sparkly fell from the ocean above. It was a shiny necklace.

"Tamatoa placed it on his shell. 'I'm beautiful!' he declared.

"From then on, Tamatoa was hooked. He searched far and wide for
other sparkly things to add to his collection, and he became more and
more obsessed with his shiny appearance.

"He stole precious items from men and from his fellow monsters, making new enemies wherever he went.

"He even crossed paths with Maui . . . though that didn't end well for Tamatoa. In the end, he escaped.

"Over the years, his collection grew and Tamatoa felt more and more powerful. He used his shininess to attract fish to eat for dinner. He became known as the most menacing scavenger of Lalotai, taking down anyone who got in his way. This meant he was often alone, but he didn't care. He only cared about one thing.

"'I'm always the most glittery one in the room,' he said.

"And when he found Maui's fishhook, which Maui had lost in the sea after his exile, Tamatoa decided it made him the most amazing—most crab-ulous—monster there ever was."

"And that's when you and Maui come in!" shouted one of the kids listening to her story.

"That's right!" Moana said. "We went to get Maui's fishhook back. Of course, we needed to be careful. Tamatoa wasn't going to let us walk away with one of his most prized possessions.

"But with some great teamwork and some shiny distractions, Maui and I were able to get the fishhook . . .

. . . and escape from Lalotai!"

"Yay!" the kids cheered.

"But what happened to Tamatoa?" one of them asked.

well, he was stuck on his back for a little while. He yelled for help, but he'd been so selfish and taken from so many of the other monsters, they began stealing from *him*.

"When Tamatoa finally got back on his claws, he had to start his collection all over again.

"Though hopefully he learned that treating others well is better than being shiny," Moana finished.

The kids nodded, agreeing with her solemnly. Then one of them raised his hand.

"Tell us another story, Moana!"

Ariel Makes Waves

Ariel was enjoying breakfast with her sisters and their father, King Triton, which was always a wonderful way to start the day together. But King Triton told his girls he wasn't able to stay, as he had to attend to ruling the kingdom.

Ariel was disappointed, because days with her father were her favorite.

But her sisters had a plan! They were going to play Ride the Current at the reef.

Once they got there, the girls counted, "One . . . two . . . three!" and flung themselves into the rushing water. Ariel, Aquata, and Andrina swam back into the current after an exciting ride, but something didn't feel right.

As they tried to move toward slower water, they realized they were stuck! They swam harder and faster, but the current was holding them in place. Not only were they caught, they were being pushed farther and farther from home.

To make matters worse, the strong current kicked up mud from the seafloor, making it impossible for them to see anything! Far from home and unable to spot the route back, the girls were lost at sea.

"How are we going to get home?" Andrina wondered aloud.

Fortunately, Ariel had an idea: if they swam up to the surface, they could look for the reef.

"We're not supposed to go there!" Aquata warned.

But Ariel knew it was their only hope, so she grabbed her sisters' hands and swam to the surface.

"Ariel! Where are you going now?" Andrina asked when Ariel started swimming toward some rocks.

"If we head over there, maybe we can rest before we search for home," she responded.

But when they got to the rocks, they found a bird. "Eek! Humans!" it screeched.

"We're not going to hurt you!" Ariel assured it. "We're mermaids, and we're lost and can't find our way home."

"Mermaids?" the bird said. "I haven't seen mermaids in years."

"Wait! You've seen mermaids before?" Aquata asked. "Do you remember where?"

"It was in a little cove that way," the bird said, pointing with its small wing.

"Then we need to go that way to get home!" Ariel said.

"I know who can help!" the bird said, then flapped away. Moments later, it was back . . . with dolphins.

"These fellows will pull you for a while."

"Oh, thank you!" Ariel said.

"I hope you get home soon!" the bird called as it flew away.

The girls held tight to the fins on the dolphins' backs while the dolphins skipped along the water and splashed through the waves.

When they got closer to the cove, the sisters thanked the dolphins for the lift and dove back into the water, hoping they were close.

But when two hulking shapes came into view, the girls froze.

"Sharks!" Ariel whispered, then swam with her sisters for the first hiding place they saw: a shipwreck.

They stopped just inside, clutching the edges of the opening and peeking at the sharks. Fortunately, the sharks started swimming farther away.

"Maybe we should stay here awhile . . . just to be safe," Andrina whispered. "Or at least *safer*."

When the girls felt safe enough to talk above a whisper, Aquata breathed a sigh of relief. "Can you imagine Attina's face when we tell her about this?"

But Ariel wasn't paying any attention—she was exploring the ship. "Ariel!" Andrina said. "What are you doing? That's *human* stuff!"

"It's wonderful!" Ariel told her sisters. She hadn't seen anything like it before.

Ariel wanted to find more, but she heard someone in the distance. *"Ariel! Aquata! Andrina!"*

"What was that?" Ariel said.

Aquata's and Andrina's eyes widened, and they all quickly swam out of the shipwreck, where two of King Triton's guards were waiting.

The king had sent them to search for his daughters when he heard they were missing.

"We came straightaway," one of the guards said, and he was impressed by the young princesses. "You've nearly made it home all by yourselves!"

But at that moment, they swam through another strong current and had to fight to move forward.

Ariel had an idea. If they swam down, they wouldn't get carried so far away.

"We're right behind you!" said one of the guards.

Ariel dove deeper into the blackness and eventually felt the pull of the current lessen. Her plan had worked!

But when she looked around, no one was with her. She was alone and lost in the darkness.

"Hello? I'm lost. Can anyone hear me?" she shouted. "I can't see anything. If only some fish could light up and show me the way . . ." she continued, talking to herself.

Just then, two lights came on, inches from her nose. It was a fish!

"Can you help me? I'm looking for my sisters and two guards," Ariel said. But the fish didn't answer. "Well, if you've seen them, could I follow you, please?"

The fish led her through tunnels until they came across a school of fish, all with lights! They lit a path for Ariel to follow, and she found her way back to the guards and her sisters. "Thank you!" Ariel called as her new friends swam away.

After everyone was reunited, it wasn't long before the girls were seated in front of their father at the palace.

"I'm overjoyed you've returned safely," he said, "but disappointed you wandered off. You could have been lost for good!"

"Your Majesty . . ." one of the guards said, "it's worth noting that when we found the princesses, they were well on their way home. Quite resourceful, I think."

"And we didn't wander off," Aquata added. "There was a strong current over the reef."

"Well," King Triton said, turning to his daughters, "I am proud that you can take care of yourselves. What would you like as a reward?"

The girls thought about it, and Ariel finally spoke up. "After breakfast tomorrow, will you come play with us on the reef?"

King Triton laughed. "There is nothing I'd like more."

Disney
Lilo & Stitch
Lilo and Stitch

In a distant, remote corner of the galaxy, Jumba Jukiba created Experiment 626, a new species. The Grand Councilwoman of the planet ordered Jumba to get rid of Experiment 626.

Just as they were about to escort 626 off to a far asteroid, he broke out. Back at the Galactic Federation headquarters, they tracked 626 as he hurtled toward an unfamiliar part of the galaxy. A control operator pinpointed 626's destination: "A planet called EE-AAR-TH." Jumba and his friend Pleakley followed 626 to Earth.

Off the small island of Kauai, a young girl named Lilo swam in
the rolling waves. When she realized she was late for hula dance class,
Lilo dashed from the ocean and tried, unsuccessfully, to slip into class
unnoticed. Her teacher wanted to know why she was all wet.

"It's Thursday. Every Thursday I take Pudge the fish a sandwich,"
Lilo said. The other students rolled their eyes. One girl, Myrtle, called
Lilo crazy. Lilo lunged at Myrtle, but the teacher caught her.

After class, Lilo forgot to wait for her older sister, Nani, and walked
home.

Not finding Lilo at the hula school, Nani rushed home to find her little sister had locked herself inside. Cobra Bubbles, a social worker, arrived at their house in time to see Nani breaking into her own home. He was evaluating Nani as a guardian for Lilo.

Lilo put on her best smile and recited the answers she and Nani had practiced. Cobra gave Lilo his business card. "Call me next time you're left here alone."

After Cobra left, Nani and Lilo got into a big fight. Later that night, Nani went to Lilo's bedroom to check on her. "We're a broken family, aren't we?" Lilo asked.

"No . . . maybe, a little. I'll tell you what, if you promise not to fight anymore, I promise not to yell at you," Nani said.

After Nani said good night, Lilo saw a shooting star and ran to make a wish. "I need someone to be my friend. Maybe send me an angel . . . the nicest angel you have," Lilo wished. Hearing Lilo's wish, Nani thought maybe Lilo could use a playmate.

Lilo didn't know the shooting star was actually 626's spaceship crash-landing in a field of sugarcane.

Next thing he knew, 626 was waking up in a kennel. Just then, Lilo and Nani entered the kennel to pick out a pet. Lilo chose 626.

Nani was shocked. "What is that thing? Does it have to be that dog?"

"Yes. He's good, I can tell. His name is . . . Stitch," Lilo said. "Can I buy him?" Nani agreed and gave Lilo two dollars.

As Lilo and Stitch left the kennel together, Jumba leapt out to capture 626, but Pleakley stopped him, reminding him they were on Earth. They couldn't use their alien technology or make themselves known.

Lilo eagerly introduced Stitch to his new home. "This is a great home. You'll like it a lot!" Lilo said. But Stitch proceeded to destroy everything in his path. Lilo objected when Nani disciplined Stitch. Nani wanted to take Stitch back to the kennel.

"He was an orphan and we adopted him!" Lilo said. "What about 'ohana? *'Ohana* means family. Family means nobody gets left behind . . .'"

"Or forgotten," Nani finished.

Lilo took Stitch up to her room. Stitch found a book about an ugly duckling. He was curious about it. Lilo explained that in the end, the duckling was happy because he knew where he belonged.

The next day, Nani
dragged Lilo and Stitch
around with her as she
went on job interviews.
Lilo used the time to
teach Stitch about her
hero, Elvis. She told
him that Elvis was a
model citizen, so he should
practice being like Elvis.
Stitch got started right
away dancing and playing
guitar, and he disrupted
every interview.

When the day drew to a close, Nani still had not gotten a job. Lilo and Stitch were sitting quietly on the beach when Nani's friend David walked up. "Hey, Lilo. Hi, Nani. How are you guys?"

"We've been having a bad day," Lilo said.

"Well, there's no better cure for a bad day than a couple of boards and some choice waves. What do you think?"

Nani agreed, and they all joined David in the sparkling water. Despite his dislike of water, Stitch became captivated by the sport, and when they returned to shore, he dragged over a board, asking for another ride.

As Lilo, Stitch, and Nani headed back out to the water, Jumba saw an opportunity to catch Stitch. While they surfed, Jumba swam up from underneath. The white water of the crashing waves hid Jumba as he pulled Stitch beneath the surface. He swam away from Jumba's grip but floundered in the waves. Fortunately, David was nearby and rescued Stitch.

Cobra had seen the whole incident and was very upset with Nani. Defeated, Nani took Lilo and Stitch home. Stitch felt guilty and hurt. He took the ugly duckling book and started walking toward the window.

"*Ohana* means family. Family means nobody gets left behind, but if you want to leave, you can. I'll remember you, though . . ." Lilo said as Stitch climbed outside. He walked deep into the forest, desperately hoping to find his own family.

The next morning, Jumba and Pleakley were back to their search for Stitch. Jumba caught up to him in the middle of the forest. Stitch told Jumba he was waiting for his family.

"You don't have one. I made you," Jumba said.

Back at the house, Lilo told Nani about Stitch. "He left. He didn't wanna be here anyway."

Nani began to console Lilo, but David arrived to announce that he had found a job for Nani. After Nani left, Stitch burst through the door. Pleakley and Jumba were not far behind. Lilo called Cobra to tell him that aliens were attacking her house. Jumba was making a mess trying to capture Stitch.

Nani returned to the house to find Cobra already there. When he saw what Stitch and Jumba had done to the house, he tried to take Lilo away.

While Nani and Cobra argued, Lilo slipped out and ran into the forest. She ran as fast as she could, trying to get as far away as she could. Stitch popped up in her path. He revealed his true alien self to her. "You're one of them?" she said.

Without warning, another alien, named Gantu, snatched up both Lilo and Stitch. Nani arrived just in time to see Gantu load them onto his ship. Stitch worked his way out of the containment pod and fell from the ship as it took off with Lilo still trapped inside. Jumba and Pleakley jumped out and contained Stitch. Nani went to confront all three of them.

"Where's Lilo? Bring her back!" Nani shouted.

Stitch shuffled over to Nani and spoke the words Lilo had taught him. "'*Ohana* means family. Family means nobody gets left behind . . .'"

"Or forgetten," Nani finished.

Everyone piled into
Jumba and Pleakley's
spaceship. Once in the
air, Jumba used his
ship to bump Gantu's
and send it spinning.

Jumba then blasted
Stitch onto Gantu's ship.
He crashed through the windshield and rescued Lilo.

"You came back!" she cried.

"Nobody gets left behind," Stitch said. Moments later, the ship
splashed into the ocean. David, who was surfing nearby, helped them
ashore, where they were met by Cobra and a fleet of aliens, including
the Grand Councilwoman.

The Grand Councilwoman wanted to take Stitch back to their home planet. Cobra stepped in. "Lilo, didn't you buy that thing at the shelter?" he asked. Lilo nodded. She approached the Grand Councilwoman, who decided to let Stitch stay with Lilo and Nani on Earth.

Nani, Lilo, and Stitch were a real family. The spirit of *'ohana* proved that anyone could belong.

Pua and Heihei

The feast to welcome spring was about to start. Moana and Gramma Tala were busy collecting shells. Moana's pet pig, Pua, tried to help, but the shells he found were never empty.

Moana was making her father a surprise gift for the feast: an anklet.

Moana strung a final shell onto the anklet, finishing it. Just then, Heihei, the foolish village rooster, ran by them wearing a part of a coconut on his head. "Silly Heihei," Moana said, removing the coconut.

Heihei turned and started pecking at Gramma's feet. "You've no more brains than a grain of sand," said Gramma, shooing him away. But he just started pecking the sand instead.

In the village, preparations for the feast had begun. While everyone was hard at work, Heihei just got in the way.

Men were busy building the *umu*, an underground oven. They piled up pieces of wood, dried husks, and coconut shells. After they started the fire, they added rocks. It wasn't long before the *umu* was hot enough to roast bananas, fish, and taro roots.

Heihei walked onto the hot rocks. "You'll set yourself on fire, you silly bird!" one man yelled, chasing him away.

Heihei ran away and stepped on a partially finished platter woven from pandan leaves. His tiny foot got trapped. But he didn't even notice as he dragged the large platter behind him.

Gramma Tala tried to catch him. But as she reached for him . . .

. . . she slipped on the
platter! Fortunately, Moana
was there to catch her.

In all the commotion,
neither of them noticed that
Moana had dropped the anklet. It
landed around Heihei's neck, and he dashed away.

"That is it!" Gramma Tala said. She wasn't giving up.

She grabbed a handwoven leaf basket and, in one fell swoop, trapped Heihei and cinched the basket shut! He hadn't seen her coming. He was too busy pecking at a rock.

But Gramma had been so focused on catching the rooster that she hadn't seen the anklet around his neck.

But Moana had just realized the anklet was missing. "Oh, no!" she said.

Just then, Pua spotted the basket. He saw Heihei's beak sticking out between the gaps in the woven leaves. When he looked closer, Pua noticed the anklet around the rooster's neck. He was determined to retrieve it for Moana.

But first Pua had to open the basket. He rolled it over and over, but that didn't work. Then Pua put the basket on top of a stick. He jumped on the stick and sent the basket flying. It fell to the ground but was still tightly shut. He had to think of another idea.

On the ground, Pua saw a long vine. He picked it up and trotted back to the basket. Pua looped the vine around the basket and dragged it along, running as fast as he could. Heihei's legs slipped out, and he ran to keep up.

Pua pulled the basket past some villagers. Because Heihei had continued to peck and peck, his head stuck out through another hole he'd made.

They passed a man cutting breadfruit. When he sliced it in half, a tasty chunk flew right into Heihei's mouth!

When Pua heard music, he knew the feast was about to begin. He dragged the basket toward a slender tree and tossed it onto a branch. Then he jumped up after it.

Pua bounced on the branch, and Heihei's basket flew into the air and then back down to the branch. The higher Pua bounced, the higher the basket flew.

Finally, Pua bounced so high that the branch flung the basket straight into him! The two animals soared through the air. Pua and Heihei squealed and clucked with glee.

When they hit the ground, the basket finally opened! Pua was thrilled. He could get the anklet to Moana! But they rolled right into a large fishing net. . . .

And they tumbled right up to Moana.

Moana untangled them and gasped when she saw the anklet around Pua's snout. "You found it!" she said, giving him a big hug.

Later that evening, Moana gave Chief Tui the anklet.

"I love it," he said.

As Moana and her father hugged, Pua heard a strange sound. It was Heihei. He couldn't cluck, because his beak was buried in a piece of driftwood, and he'd gotten tangled up in pieces of the basket again.

Fortunately, Pua was ready to help him again.

Night Games

Nemo was enjoying the perfect afternoon. He was playing tag with his octopus friend Pearl. The two friends chased each other from sponge bed to sponge bed.

"Tag, you're it!" Pearl giggled as she tapped Nemo on the back. "Bet you can't catch me!"

Nemo flipped his fins faster and chased Pearl past the edge of the sponge beds. He was just about to tag her when he spotted something tall and wide up ahead.

"What *is* that?" he shouted, pointing a fin over Pearl's head.

Nemo swam toward the looming object. It seemed to wave at them in the gentle current.

"W-wait for me!" Pearl called out.

Getting closer, Nemo yelped with excitement. It was a huge seaweed bed! The bed was a giant maze of green and red seaweed. Some spots were almost too dense to swim through, while others formed small pockets of open space. Pearl and Nemo had never seen it before!

"This looks like the perfect hide-and-seek spot!" Nemo said to Pearl. "Want to play?"

Pearl looked around nervously. The sea had started to turn dark. "I would love to, Nemo, but I think we should head home. It's getting late, and both our dads will be wondering where we are."

Nemo realized Pearl was right. It was time to go home for the night.

When Nemo got back to his sea anemone, his father was waiting.
They had dinner, and Nemo told him all about his afternoon playing
with Pearl and finding the seaweed bed.

"That sounds like a neat place," Marlin told his son. "But now it's
time for bed."

"Aww, come on, Dad," Nemo protested. "Can't I just stay up a little
bit longer?"

Marlin shook his head. "Try to get some sleep, Son."

Nemo settled into bed and closed his eyes. He told himself a long bedtime story. He thought about boring things, like math class. He even counted dolphins. But he still wasn't sleepy.

Finally, Nemo got up and swam to his father. "Dad, I can't fall asleep. I've tried, but I just can't, so I was thinking . . ."

Marlin looked up at his son. He had a pretty good idea what Nemo had been thinking. "What exactly were you thinking, Son?" he asked anyway.

Nemo could not stop thinking about his fun day.

"I think you and I should go to the seaweed bed now. That way you'll know it's safe, and I can go there tomorrow and play with my friends. I promise, when we get back, I'll go right to bed. Please?" Nemo begged.

Marlin looked at his son's hopeful face. Seeing the seaweed bed for himself *did* seem like a good idea. "All right," he said finally. "Let's go take a look at this new find of yours."

"Yes!" Nemo shouted, flipping over in excitement. "Let's go!"

As Marlin and Nemo swam through the reef, Nemo realized he was glad to have his father with him.

Squinting, Nemo looked for the seaweed bed. But in the dark, it was impossible to see anything.

"Son," Marlin began, "are you sure the bed is out this far?"

Nemo wasn't sure. He was just about to give up when he saw a light in the distance. The speck drew closer and brighter until it lit up the water all around Nemo and Marlin. In the middle of the light was the strangest fish Nemo had ever seen.

The new fish had giant lights under her eyes.

"Hi, I'm . . . I'm Nemo," Nemo stammered, amazed.

"Hi!" the other fish said. "I'm Lumen."

"It's nice to meet you, Lumen," Marlin said. "I'm Nemo's dad. How come we've never seen you before?"

Lumen fluttered around, causing her light to waver and flicker. "My family and I are nocturnal," she said. "We swim and play at night while everyone else is sleeping."

"Dad and I are being nightturnal, too!" Nemo said. "We're looking for this big seaweed bed I found this afternoon. Do you know where it is?"

"You bet I do!" Lumen said. "That's where I live. Follow me!"

Lumen led Nemo and Marlin to the seaweed bed. "Do you want to play a game?" she asked.

"Yeah!" Nemo shouted. "Can we, Dad? Please?"

Marlin nodded. "Just stay out here in the open," he said. "I'm going to go have a look around."

While the kids played, Marlin explored the seaweed bed to make sure it was safe. Behind him, he could hear his son counting down from one hundred.

"Don't peek!" Marlin heard Lumen shout as she swam off to find a good hiding place.

Marlin pushed through the maze of thick green and red strands, swimming farther and farther into the seaweed bed. Suddenly, he realized how dark and quiet it had become. He could no longer hear Nemo or see Lumen's light!

Marlin spun around. He had no idea where he was! All he could see was seaweed. He was lost!

"Nemo!" he shouted. "Nemo! Where are you?" But there was no answer. Flipping his fins, Marlin tried to find his way out.

Just when he was beginning to think he would be stuck in the seaweed bed forever, Marlin spotted a faint light in the distance.

Following the light, Marlin made his way through the seaweed until he finally hit the open water. There, right where he'd left them, were Nemo and Lumen.

Marlin sighed in relief.

"Dad!" Nemo said. "There you are! We didn't know where you'd gone! Don't you know better than to go swimming off by yourself in the dark?"

Marlin smiled. "I guess I should have followed my own advice!"

Nemo gave Marlin a hug. "I'm just glad we found you, Dad."

Together, the two said good night to Lumen. As they swam home, Marlin yawned.

Nemo looked at his father. "When we get home, I think you should go right to bed, Dad," Nemo said with a teasing look in his eye. "You've had more than enough adventure for one day."

Ariel and the Whale Song

"Ariel!" called someone from beneath the water. Ariel dove into the sea and found her friend Flounder waiting for her.

"Hello, Flounder," she said. "Isn't the water lovely today?"

"Yes, Ariel, but we should be getting back to Sebastian," Flounder said. Sebastian had organized a special concert for the first day of summer. Ariel was sure Sebastian would be setting up for it already. She was also sure that he would *not* be happy if she was late.

Ariel and Flounder swam side by side toward home. Ariel admired the beautiful coral reef as they passed it.

"Ah!" came a shout from beside her. Flounder was quivering and covering his eyes.

"Oh, Flounder, it's just a little crab," Ariel assured him. She peeled Flounder's fins away from his eyes as the crab scuttled away. Flounder breathed a sigh of relief.

"We need to toughen you up a bit." Ariel smiled and gently prodded him with her elbow. She loved her friend, but even she knew he was a bit of a scaredy-fish.

Ariel and Flounder finally reached Sebastian, who was leading the orchestra through the final song of the concert. Why was Sebastian rushing through the rehearsal?

"Sebastian," Ariel said with a laugh, "slow down. We have plenty of time to get ready."

"But, Princess, we don't," Sebastian told her. "This is a concert we are performing for the whales. They are migrating through Coral Cove today."

Ariel had always wanted to meet a whale! But how could she meet one if she was singing at the concert?

"The concert will be perfect!" Ariel assured Sebastian as she started to swim away.

"Where are you going?" Sebastian cried.

"I just need to get something from my treasure grotto," Ariel said, thinking quickly. "I promise I'll be back before the concert!" And with that she swam off, with Flounder following close behind.

"All right, Flounder. Are you up for a quick trip to Coral Cove?" Ariel asked with a sly smile.

"Coral Cove? But . . . but why are you going there?" Flounder asked.

"To meet the whales," she told him. "They never visit us at the palace, so this is my only chance."

Soon they reached the edge of the reef, where Coral Cove began.

Even Ariel felt a little nervous entering uncharted waters.

And was it just her, or had it actually gotten colder?

"I—I don't see any whales here," Flounder stammered.

"Me neither . . ." Ariel said, slightly
disappointed. She looked around, hoping to
see some sort of sign of the whales. But
instead of seeing a sign, she heard one.

Ariel listened carefully. The noise seemed to be coming from above. It sounded like a song!

"Flounder, follow me!" Ariel said. She swam quickly toward the brilliant light that broke through the ocean's surface. The tune was getting louder. But Flounder noticed a dark shape below them.

Ariel arrived at the surface, hoping to find whatever was making the beautiful song. As she looked around, she saw nothing but the wide, flat ocean.

She frowned, disappointed. Then she looked for Flounder. Where had her friend gone?

She was about to dive back under when Flounder suddenly burst into the air.

"It was—it was a shark!" Flounder cried.

Ariel tried to calm her friend. "Flounder, sharks don't come into these waters, remember? It's too close to land for them," Ariel told him. Then she gasped. Something was approaching them, and it sure *looked* like a shark. Ariel dove beneath the water to get a better look.

It came closer and closer until it was so close that Ariel could make out a giant tail. But before she could figure out who the tail belonged to, it made a giant swooping motion, and an underwater wave surrounded Ariel and Flounder with bubbles!

When the bubbles cleared, Ariel was amazed at what she saw.

It was a mama whale and her baby. And they were singing!

"Whale song," Ariel whispered.

Ariel and Flounder floated next to the whales for a few moments, knowing they might never get so close again. Ariel listened carefully to the melody. Then she sang it back to them. The whales smiled at her and continued to sing the tune, and Ariel joined in.

Suddenly, the two whales headed straight toward the ocean's surface and burst into the air. They belly flopped onto the sea. The huge waves sent Ariel and Flounder soaring into the air.

When they landed back in the water, they both had to catch their breath. Then they burst into laughter.

Ariel smiled. It had been an amazing afternoon. But it was time to get back home.

Ariel and Flounder arrived just in time for the concert. When it was time for Ariel's solo, she decided to make a change. She belted out the beautiful whale song she had learned from the mama and baby whale.

As she continued to sing, she could feel the water's currents change, and she knew the whales were passing by. She smiled and sang even louder to celebrate the start of summer *and* to honor her new friends.

The Ghost-Light Fish

"**H**ave a great day, Nemo!" Marlin the clownfish said as he hugged his son good-bye. He and Dory, a regal blue tang fish, were dropping Nemo off at school.

"All right!" Nemo exclaimed. "I will . . . just as soon as you let go."

Marlin realized he was still hugging his son. "Oh, right!" Marlin said with a chuckle. He let go.

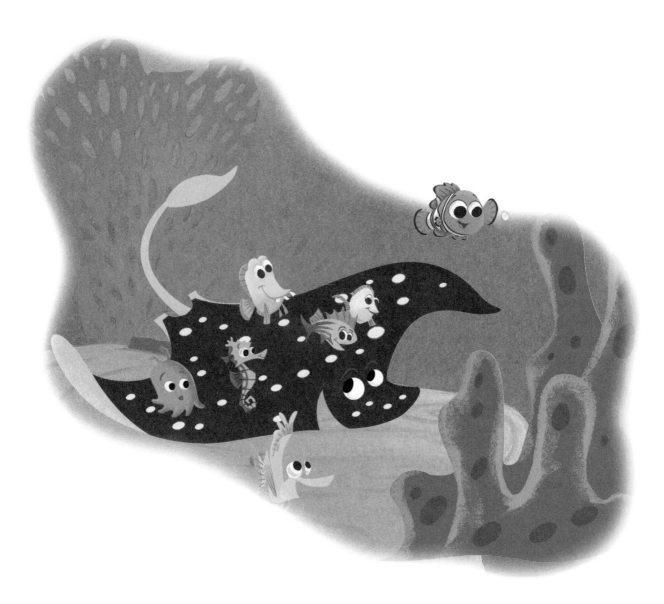

Nemo swam off to join the other students and their teacher, Mr. Ray.
"Bye, Dad!" the little clownfish called out. "Bye, Dory! See you later!"
Nemo loved school. So did his friends Tad the long-nosed butterfly
fish, Pearl the octopus, and Sheldon the seahorse. How could they not
when Mr. Ray made everything so much fun?

Mr. Ray took his students exploring all over the reef. Every day, Nemo and his classmates got an up-close look at different kinds of sea life.

That day, Mr. Ray was taking them to a clearing on the ocean floor.

"Okay, explorers," Mr. Ray said when they arrived, "now it's time to do a little searching on your own. Let's see if each of you can find a shell. Then we'll identify them together!"

The youngsters fanned out. Nemo searched in the shadow of some coral. Pearl peeked into a bit of algae. Sheldon headed to search the sand.

Tad was the first of Nemo's friends to find something. "Hey, guys!" he cried. "Look at this!"

Nemo, Pearl, and Sheldon swam over to their friend.

They crowded around and stared in wonder at the gleaming white shell Tad held in his fin.

"Coooooool," said Sheldon.

"It's so pretty," Pearl said. "Where did you find it?"

Tad pointed to a cave. "In there," he said. "Maybe there are more!" Tad darted toward the cave entrance.

"Yeah!" said Pearl, following him. "I want to find one, too."

"Me too!" cried Sheldon. "Are you coming, Nemo?" he asked.

"Nah," Nemo replied. "You guys go on." He wanted to find a shell that was different from everybody else's.

Only a few minutes passed before Nemo heard an odd noise. He looked up and saw Sheldon, Tad, and Pearl bolting out of the cave at full speed, screaming loudly.

"What's the matter?" Nemo asked. "Is it a barracuda? An eel?"

Sheldon shook his head. "No, worse!" he said. "It's a g-g-ghost fish!"

"Yeah, right," Nemo replied. Then he noticed Tad's fin was empty. "Where's your shell?" he asked.

Tad looked down. "Aw, shucks," he said. "I was going to give it to my mom." Then he peered into the cave. "I must have dropped it in there. But I'm not going back for it. Not with that ghost fish on the loose!"

"Don't worry," Nemo told Tad. "I'll find your shell."

The little clownfish swam bravely into the cave.

See? he said to himself. *Nothing to be afraid of.*

Just then, Nemo froze. On the cave wall next to him was a huge, fish-shaped shadow!

Nemo took a deep breath. "Uh, excuse me, Mr. Ghost Fish? Or is it Ms. Ghost Fish?"

"A ghost fish?!" someone with a tiny voice said. "Where? Where? Don't let it get me!"

The ghost fish didn't *sound* very scary. Nemo swam closer to the shadow. "Are *you* afraid of ghost fish?" he asked it.

"Yeah!" squeaked the little voice. "Who isn't?"

Nemo followed the voice. There, cowering behind a rock, was a little fish, glowing softly with pale orange light. The ghost fish wasn't a ghost fish at all! It was just a glow-in-the-dark fish. Its glow had shone on an oddly shaped piece of coral and made a spooky-looking shadow!

Nemo's fear was forgotten. "Oh, hi!" he called out.

Startled, the glowing fish darted behind another rock. Then, timidly, he peeked out from behind it to study Nemo.

"Don't be afraid," Nemo said. "I'm just a little fish—like you." He smiled. "My name's Nemo. What's yours?"

The fish swam out cautiously. "Eddy," he replied, his eyes still wide. "You mean there's no ghost fish?"

Nemo chuckled. "I thought *you* were the ghost fish!" He explained the whole funny story.

"By the way," said Nemo, "how do you glow like that?"

Eddy shrugged. "I just do," he replied. "My whole family does."

Nemo thought of someone who would know more about Eddy's glow: Mr. Ray! So Nemo invited Eddy to meet his teacher and his friends. Then, swimming out of the cave together, the two little fish laughed about the way they had met.

"You really thought *I* was a ghost fish?" Eddy asked with a giggle.

Outside, Nemo rejoined his friends. "Sorry I didn't find your shell," Nemo said to Tad. "But I did find your ghost fish!"

Then Nemo and Eddy told their tale. Before long, Nemo's friends' fear of the ghost fish was forgotten, too. Everyone wanted to know more about Eddy!

"Can you glow different colors?" Pearl asked.

"How come the water doesn't put out your light?" questioned Tad. Nemo wanted to know what made Eddy glow.

"Good question, Nemo," Mr. Ray replied. "See these patches on either side of Eddy's jaw? Inside them are teeny-tiny glow-in-the-dark organisms. When you see Eddy glow, you're really seeing those organisms glow."

Everyone oohed and aahed over Eddy's glow patches.

Eddy led the whole class into the cave to show them his glow-in-the-dark world—including his family. Nemo thought it was one of the most beautiful things he had ever seen. But there was still one thing weighing on his mind.

"Mr. Ray," Nemo whispered to his teacher, "I didn't finish the assignment. I mean, I didn't find a shell."

Mr. Ray laughed. "That's okay, Nemo," he replied. "I'd say you still get an A in exploring for today!"

Wave Rider

One morning, Moana and Gramma Tala went for a walk on their favorite Motunui beach. They watched as some of the village children tried to ride the ocean waves.

"I wish I could do that," Moana said. "Tell me the story, Gramma. Please?"

Gramma Tala laughed and sat down with Moana.

"When I was young, I was a lot like you. I loved being by the water. I would run to it whenever I could, playing and dancing with the waves."

"You still do," said Moana.

"Yes, I still do. Now quiet down and listen.

"My friends the manta rays would join me and I would watch them ride the waves, their bodies gracefully sailing across each crest. Sometimes, I would try to do it, too, right along with them. We would glide along the water, and all I could hear and see was the ocean and the sky.

"One day, while I was out playing with the rays, a big wave tossed me onto the sand like a sea cucumber! It was only when I heard laughter that I realized I was not alone—all my friends were there, watching me!

"But the only one who didn't laugh was Asolelei, the wood-carver.

"I didn't want to be laughed at, but oh, how I wanted to ride those waves! So, whenever I could, I'd sneak out to the water and try again. And again. Then I'd wipe out and get right back to it!

"Then one evening, something happened that changed everything. A bird appeared in the distance. It looked like it was standing on the water! As it came closer, I could see it was on a piece of driftwood. I admired the beautiful bird as it rode the wave, perfectly poised. It sped by me, the wind ruffling its feathers. I took one last look and I knew—I had to do that!

"The next morning, I started searching for something to ride on. I tried everything I could find: bark, banana leaves, paddles, and empty turtle shells. But most of the time I would just fall right off. And even when I was able to stay on, everything quickly bent, broke, or sunk.

"But I kept on, for days. No one could make me lose focus or stop me from trying. I was determined to feel like that bird.

"Then one night, as I watched Asolelei carving by the fire, I had an idea . . . I could make a board!

"I drew a design in the sand, and Asolelei agreed to help me. He patiently showed me how to carve, sand, and polish the wood.

"It took a lot of hard work, but soon my board was ready. It was so beautiful and I couldn't wait to try it. So early one morning, I took it to the ocean.

"I paddled out as far as I dared. Then I floated on it, waiting for the right wave. I knew I had to be patient.

"When a good wave came, I went for it. Did I ride it to the shore?
Of course not! The people who were watching me were probably
saying, 'Crazy, crazy Tala. Give it up already!'

"But when I saw the rays, I knew I couldn't give up on something that I felt so strongly about in my heart.

"When the next good wave approached, I was ready. Slowly, I stood up—poised and balanced—and the wave carried me across the water with the wind in my feathers, just like that bird!"

"You don't have feathers, Gramma," Moana said, giggling.

"I did that day, Moana. Oh, I had wings! I didn't even notice my friends watching until they cheered. And the loudest of them all was Asolelei . . . your grandfather."

Moana clapped her hands. "I love that story!"

Gramma Tala smiled. "I do, too." She handed Moana the board she and Asolelei had carved all those years before. "Are you ready to give it a try?"

Moana's eyes widened as she grabbed the board. "Yes!"

Gramma Tala followed Moana as she ran toward the water.

Moana paddled into the ocean next to her grandmother.

When Gramma Tala saw the look on her granddaughter's face, she knew Moana would continue to try again and again, no matter how many times she wiped out.

It wasn't long before the day came when
Gramma Tala and Moana flew across the
water, like birds of a feather, together.